Ellie for President

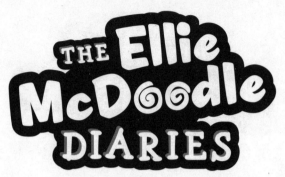

THE Ellie McDoodle DIARIES

by Ruth McNally Barshaw

Have Pen, Will Travel

New Kid in School

Best Friends Fur-Ever

Most Valuable Player

The Show Must Go On

Ellie for President

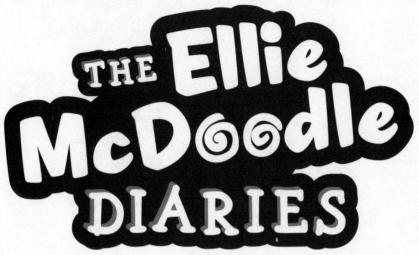

THE Ellie McDoodle DIARIES

Ellie for President

WRITTEN AND ILLUSTRATED BY

Ruth McNally Barshaw

BLOOMSBURY
NEW YORK   LONDON   NEW DELHI   SYDNEY

To those who take a risk, those who play fair,
and those who try hard when it isn't easy

First published in the United States of America in September 2014
by Bloomsbury Children's Books
www.bloomsbury.com

Bloomsbury is a registered trademark of Bloomsbury Publishing Plc

For information about permission to reproduce selections from this book, write to
Permissions, Bloomsbury Children's Books, 1385 Broadway, New York, New York 10018
Bloomsbury books may be purchased for business or promotional use. For information on bulk
purchases please contact Macmillan Corporate and Premium Sales Department at
specialmarkets@macmillan.com

Library of Congress Cataloging-in-Publication Data
Barshaw, Ruth McNally, author, illustrator.
The Ellie McDoodle diaries : Ellie for president / by Ruth McNally Barshaw.
pages   cm.
Summary: Ellie McDoodle is excited about starting a school newspaper and serving as editor, so when her friends
and family convince her to run for class president—against her new crush, Jake—she is disappointed to have to give
up the job temporarily, but is soon caught up in making posters and speeches and getting to know Jake better.
ISBN 978-1-61963-061-1 (hardcover) • ISBN 978-1-61963-234-9 (e-book)
[1. School newspapers—Fiction. 2. Politics, Practical—Fiction. 3. Elections—Fiction.
4. Friendship—Fiction. 5. Schools—Fiction. 6. Family life—Fiction.] I. Title. II. Title: Ellie for president.
PZ7.B28047Enf 2014   [Fic]—dc23   2014005605

Typeset in Casino Hand
Art created with a Sanford Uni-ball Micro pen
Book design by Yelena Safronova

Printed and bound in the U.S.A. by Thomson-Shore Inc., Dexter, Michigan
2 4 6 8 10 9 7 5 3 1

It's Grandpa George's birthday party—time to celebrate the craziness that makes my family fun. Grandpa loves every part of it, even my cousin's song:

Happy birthday to you. You live in a zoo. You look like a hagfish, and you smile like one too!

Mom, Dad, Risa, Josh, and Ben-Ben

My best friend, Mo

Cousins, aunts, and uncles

Lots more joking follows:

What a gigantic fire—you'll never be able to blow out all those candles.

I'm ready with the fire extinguisher!

We're ready with the garden hose!

Grandpa winks at me, takes a big breath, and blows out the candles.

Ben-Ben helps.

Ew.

Of course these are trick candles that keep relighting themselves. Then Grandma Joan hands Grandpa a knife to cut the cake and—

Scrape!

Cheezers! Grandpa can't cut it!

Bring me a hacksaw!

It's not a cake! It's just a cake pan turned over and decorated. The laughter is deafening. Mom fooled all of us. Next Mom brings out the real cake. It's easy to cut.

I'm capturing the whole scene in this book, and I draw it for Grandpa as a birthday present.

Oh, Ellie, what a gesture.

Keep drawing. Keep sharing your art.

You forgot to sign it.

Oops! Let me add that.

I love your pictures, Ellie. I wish you could teach me how to draw better.

While everyone watches I give my cousins a little art lesson.

Just look for the shapes in things.

Pretty soon we're all drawing dragons lighting birthday candles.

Mom says it's a school day tomorrow and we have to go home, but everyone wants to keep drawing. Grandpa thinks of a solution:

You send your cartoons and art lessons to me, and I'll make sure the whole family gets them.

Then it's a hugfest good night and we head home.

The next day Mo tells practically the whole school about Grandpa's birthday party and Mom's cake prank. She acts out the whole thing. Mo is very dramatic.

Check out Ellie's drawings of it!

Now EVERYONE wants to see my sketch journal. Part of me loves this. Part of me feels like throwing up. I don't like being the center of attention THIS much.

Then of course the worst possible thing happens. Someone snatches my book and runs!!!

In Mrs. Whittam's English class my friends bombard me with notes.

To Ellie—I'm sorry Shane took your diary. He's a joker, always goofing around. —Jake

Everybody likes your art! Very cool! —Daquon

Jake is a hero! ♡ Mo

I ♡ your art. ♡ Yasmeen

We should figure out how to publish your art. —Travis

Did you notice how Jake looked at you when he rescued your book? —Sitka

I sign to Travis with my fingers: I'm not that good! Oops. Mrs. Whittam is watching. She can read sign language. I hide my notes and my fingers.

Mr. Brendall's science class is more like an art class today. We're drawing butterflies, then coloring them to match something on the classroom walls—posters, bulletin boards, anything.

I ♡ 🦋's

It's all about camouflage: how well do they fit in? And that makes me wonder, is it better to blend in or stand out?

Daquon, Mo, Travis, Yasmeen, Sitka, and I are the FOES, the Friends of Epic Sagacity (which means wisdom). Today we gather at my house after school to hang out. I'm drawing, like always.

You should put your art on a blog!

What?

A journal on the Internet.

Risa is spying on us.

You'd better get Mom and Dad's permission first.

Oops.
Okay.
Done.

Mom gives permission with two rules:
1. She gets to see any blog pages and also any reader comments before they're published.
2. This project can't interfere with my schoolwork.

I draw up my first comic to put on the blog.

Hello! I'm Ellie McDoodle. My real name is Ellie McDougal, but my friends nicknamed me because I draw a lot.

I'm always looking for new things to draw.

Let me hear from you!

My nose sniffs out new stories.

I am handy with a pen.

Cheezers! I like to play with words.

I am five feet tall.

Grandpa will like this. I think my cousins and friends will also. I'm not putting a comic about Jake's rescue on my blog. That's <u>way</u> too personal. If the whole world can see whatever is online, I'm not sharing personal stuff.

I draw up a couple of art lessons—

—and get Mom's approval.

Then we scan in the art and
put it on my new blog.

I'm published!!!

I send my blog link to Grandpa. A minute later
he calls me and e-mails me at the same time.

Ellie! This is marvelous!
Your art and writing are a force. Use it wisely.

While we're talking, Mom approves two comments
on my blog. Grandpa has already shared my art link
with the rest of the family. This is AMAZING! It's
an art show on my computer.

I look at the world differently now. No matter what I see, I find myself thinking, can this go on my blog?

The FOES leave at dinnertime and I feel bad that I'm glad to see them go. It means I can draw.

This is my house if I were a stinkbug on the wall:

These male creatures smell bad to a person, but to a bug they smell good.

These two smell like flowers. To a bee they'd smell yummy.

He smells pretty gross. He just got home from the gym.

This girl smells like ink and paper. We bugs avoid her.

After Mom snorts and approves it, I add this art to my blog. Ding!! Mom approves a sweet comment from Grandma Joan. I love getting comments!

The next day in school Mrs. Whittam is talking about the history of communications.

"How we talk to each other might be the first thing to change to fit an adapting society's needs. Look back to the start of cave paintings, campfire stories, running messengers, Pony Express, the printing press, telegraph, telephone, mail, radio, satellite, e-mail, text messaging . . . And it will continue to evolve. Tomorrow text messaging will be old. Blogs are replacing newsletters."

Mo tells Mrs. Whittam about my blog.
Mrs. Whittam wants to see it, so we pull it up on the classroom computer.

Now _everyone_ wants a blog.
Daquon shows our class how to do it.

"Get permission from your family _first_! If they say it's okay and you set up a blog with your work and send me the link, I'll give you extra credit."

Mrs. Whittam adds: "Please don't expect a lot of comments on your work. Ellie has a big family, a big support group."

At lunch we FOES talk about blogging.

We should do one together.

It could be like a magazine of all our cool stuff.

Yeah! Mo's photos, my jokes, Sitka's poetry, Yasmeen's short stories . . .

Daquon's amazing travel adventures, Ellie's comics . . .

We could actually print it!

We could sell copies! We could make money doing this!

17

If we want to sell a lot of copies, this has to be a really great magazine.

We should put something BIG and important on the front page.

Something nobody expects to see.

Hmm. Principal Ping!

YES!!!

Draw Principal Ping and make it funny. THAT will get attention for sure!

I don't answer because I am already drawing.

I'm not worried. This is my best art. Everyone will see it, and I want them all to laugh.

After school Yasmeen pulls the FOES into Mr. Brendall's classroom to help clean animal cages.

I'm cuddling a degu, a rodent from Chile.

I'm letting the hermit crabs use my hands as a treadmill.

While we work we show Mr. Brendall our project, four pages filled with cool stuff by the FOES. He calls it a literary magazine, and shows us the one he and his friends made when they were in college.

To thank us for helping with his animals, Mr. Brendall offers to print 50 copies of our magazine for us.

Daquon jokes, "We should sell them for a thousand dollars each. We'll be rich!"

We all laugh. No one would pay that much.

I'm a little worried. Everyone <u>liked</u> my art, but I'm not sure if they <u>loved</u> it. I swear Mo can read my mind.

Mo: It's fine. It's more than fine. Your art is fantastic, fantabulous, fruitalicious!

Me: Um, fruitalicious?

Mo: It's a word I made up. It means juiced up with super greatness.

Okay. My art is fruitalicious.

The next morning I find out that I shouldn't have worried. The magazine sells out in five seconds. EVERYONE is laughing at my art of Principal Ping.

We need to print more copies.

Travis, Mo, and I ask Ms. Trebuchet, the art teacher, to print some for us.

At first she gives us the stink-eye when she finds out we're going to sell them.

We are not too proud to beg.

It's for a good cause!

It's for a new playground!

There's a LOT of art in it!

Well, I like the art, but Principal Ping might not.

She prints 150 more copies. And you are not going to believe this: WE SELL THEM ALL!! Our plan for a new playground is going to work, 25 cents at a time. It'll take a while, but it'll be worth it.

Here are the words I have heard people use to describe the magazine:

awesome ~~HHt HHt~~ ~~HHt~~

cool ~~HHt~~ ~~HHt~~ ~~HHt~~ |||

amazing ||||

good ~~HHt~~ ~~HHt~~ ||

sweet ~~HHt~~ ||

it rocks |

epic |||

stupendous |

bizarre |

fun ~~HHt~~ |||

creative |

hilarious ||

funny ~~HHt~~ ~~HHt~~

super-dee- ~~HHt~~ ~~HHt~~ |
duper

slanted |
(wait—what does
THAT mean?)

fruitalicious |
(Mo)

This is magnificently beneficial. Add these to your list. And also it's lugubrious.

Thanks, Shane.

a sensory delight with a smooth bouquet |
(somebody's been watching too many commercials)

I feel like I can fly! The giddy happiness lasts exactly seven and a half minutes. As I walk into Mr. Brendall's science class, Principal Ping's voice comes over the announcement system.

Mr. Brendall, please send Ellie McDougal down to see me.

Everyone looks at me.

Oooooooo! You're in trouble!

Maybe I AM in trouble!

Instant dread. I take the back stairs to the principal's office. That's the long way.

Principal Ping is smiling. I spy our magazine on her desk. Suddenly I feel like a fly—she is the spider. She starts weaving her web.

"I like that you students have started a school newspaper. Some features are very well done."

Not the art, I bet.

All her jewelry looks like daggers.

"I think our students would like to see more."

More?

"Yes. And our fifth-grade teacher, Mr. Z, has agreed to help."

Mr. Z?

Mr. Z stands up, practically knocking out the ceiling. I'm embarrassed I didn't notice him earlier.

> Hi, Ellie. Our school is starting a newspaper club and you can be editor in chief and editorial cartoonist. Our first meeting is today after school. Bring your friends.

"That sounds perfect, Mr. Z. You'll find Ellie is a hard worker who always follows the rules."

Her eyes narrow into little slits. I shiver. It's not even cold in here.

"Isn't that right, Ellie?"

Um, right?

> Nice to meet you.

Cheezers. What just happened? And is it okay?
And how do I feel about it?
    I'm not sure.

I rejoin my science class and ask the FOES what they think about Mr. Z and the newspaper idea. I'm surprised that they like it.

Let's do it.

Let's at least try. Maybe it'll be fun.

You might be surprised.

Mr. Z was my favorite teacher.

Mine too!

I had him for fifth-grade English and history.

He was my basketball coach. He played in college and in Italy. He's cool. You'll see.

The FOES and a few other friends go with me to Mr. Z's classroom after school for his meeting. There are 30 kids here from the fourth, fifth, and sixth grades. Man, this idea grew fast!

Think of a name for the newspaper. The contest starts now.

He introduces me as editor in chief.

Each of the FOES is put in charge of something.
I can see why everyone likes Mr. Z so much. I'm
in charge of interviews, and I'll also draw some
editorial cartoons about life at King Elementary.

This will be fun!

Mo's in charge
of photos.

my to-do lists
from Mr. Z

Mr. Z gives each of us something to work on for
the first issue. My job is to interview Principal
Ping. I'm a little nervous about it. Scratch that. I
am a LOT nervous. I probably should tell her I don't
plan to draw a mean comic about her.

At home that night, I work on my Principal Ping interview. My family tries to help. They're, um, not very helpful.

Risa: Ask what hair products she uses.

Mom: Ask her what life was like when she was a kid.

Me: I don't want to remind her of my art.

Josh: Ask her this: Did you never have a sense of humor, or did you lose it when you became a principal?

Me: Thanks.

Dinnertime comes fast. Risa suggests that we vote: carry out or go to a restaurant. Dad vetoes the restaurant though. We'll do carryout because Ben-Ben is being such a monkey boy.

Josh gets gross: Which is more disgusting, a hagfish or a baby fulmar?

Me: What's a fulmar?

Josh: It looks like a seagull.

Me: Aw! That's not disgusting. That's cute.

Josh: A hagfish slimes itself to escape predators. Then it ties itself in a knot to clean off the slime. The baby fulmar throws up on predators.

Me: I'm not hungry anymore.

Risa: If your conversation makes me throw up, is that more disgusting than a hagfish?

Josh: Bring it up and we'll vote on it.

I decide to go with Dad to pick up the food while they stay here. And also, ick.

When we return from the restaurant there's
a surprise. As I'm getting to the table, something
terrifying rushes my legs. It isn't human.

It's Principal Ping!

I mean, Mrs. Claus!

Josh and Risa have decorated one of Mom's
Santa statues (well, it's Mrs. Claus) and put her
on wheels.

Normal Mrs. Claus

Mrs. Claus dressed up as Principal Ping

I am totally freaked out. Everyone laughs at my scream.

All my friends think my family is crazy because of how we scare each other with Mrs. Claus. (They're right. We ARE crazy. It's kind of a weird tradition.)

I think seeing her as Principal Ping will give me nightmares.

remote control

Everyone leaps to catch the food.

Whew. No more excitement, please. Dinner. Bedtime. Good night.

Last night my fortune cookie said, "You must first experience failure before you can enjoy success." That's such a cheery thought.

Heading into my interview with Principal Ping, I am thinking more about failure than anything else. Weirdly, though, the interview goes great. I start with some easy questions to puff her up.

"What surprises you about your job?"

How many different hats I have to wear.

I suddenly envision Principal Ping in the world's goofiest pile of hats.

She lists a gazillion duties and ends with
student government. I haven't heard anything
about that before, so I ask what her plans are.

P. Ping: I'm going to announce class officer
elections for fourth, fifth, and sixth grades soon.
Me: Whoa! Hey, if I am careful how I write
it up, can you announce the elections in the
newspaper instead of over the speakers?

I can barely sit still.

P. Ping: Hmm. Very well, but only if your
newspaper can come out tomorrow.
Me: I think we're done here! Thank you!

I interrupt Mr. Z's class as soon as the interview ends. I have to give him the election news.

Mr. Z: FABULOUS!! That's new news! It's a scoop! Spread the word to meet in the library after school. Getting this first edition out tomorrow will take a <u>lot</u> of hard work. Think we can do it?

Yes!!

When I get back to class Mr. Brendall lets me announce our newspaper deadline.

Mo jumps into action: "I'll take photos of Mr. Brendall's classroom animals, and we'll run a contest to think of funny captions for them!"

Sitka already has a whole page full of poetry contributions.

All of the things we thought up for our magazine, we can do for our newspaper. Also, a lot of other kids want to contribute stuff. This will be a really thick edition.

By the time we meet Mr. Z in the library, I am excited to announce we have the entire newspaper figured out and we have plenty of extras for next week's edition.

WONDERFUL! Scoop McDoodle: that's my new name for you. Brilliantly done, all of you. I'm so proud of you!

And Ellie, as editor you will go over what everyone else creates to see if they can improve it—I'll help too.

Mr. Z gives us a quick lesson on how to write articles and how to fit photos, artwork, and articles into a page layout that's easy to read.

Mr. Z says:

- Say the important stuff up front: who, what, why, when, where, how.
- If you have a good idea, act on it. Don't wait.
- Take really good notes.
- Trim unnecessary stuff.

Another job for me: design the masthead, the newspaper name art.

We vote on a list of names:

King's Corner, Let Freedom Ring,
The Dream, The Mane Event,
The Cub Reporter . . .
Deborah's idea wins.

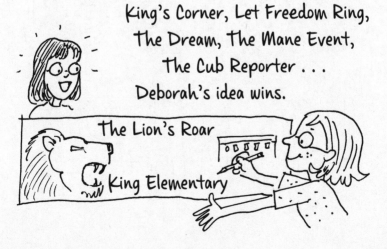

The Lion's Roar

King Elementary

When we're done, we all huddle and stretch our hands into the middle.

Mr. Z says, "Excellence!"

We all repeat, "EXCELLENCE!!!"

Mr. Z says we will do that a lot but with a different word every time. "Newspaper people need to use a variety of sparkle words."

A lot of my friends are here. I'm especially glad to see Jake.

Before walking home we FOES talk on the lawn by the lion, our regular meeting place.

Cheezers. I'm not the president sort.

At dinner I'm just minding my own business laughing at Josh and Risa's jokes, when Dad says,

I vote we make Ellie the leader of tonight's family game.

Who, me?

You don't have to be perfect at it. Just do your best, Ellie.

You're GREAT at being imperfect!

That's for sure.

New Mrs. Claus in the works

Okay, fine. I invent a game, Advance McDougal.

It involves a sponge ball, a fan, lots of questions, and three dice.

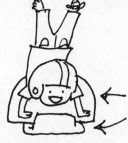

I made these game pieces from photos and clay.

Ben-Ben gets to do a somersault and run around the room every time someone scores a point.

For extra credit, Josh has to write a rhyme about a sport that Dad names and he has to include color words from Mom and a challenge for Risa.

I direct it all. After three exhausting rounds, Risa calls me "a surprisingly good leader."

The next morning we're excited to see what everyone thinks about our newspaper.

It's a much bigger deal than our magazine was. Principal Ping mentions it in the morning announcements. Everyone in the whole school will read it. And a lot of people worked on it.

Mrs. Whittam says, "Will those who worked on The Lion's Roar please stand?"

A LOT stand—like, half of the room!

The other half of the room applauds. I have to admit, it feels pretty awesome to be treated like a rock star.

In history class we look at the history of elections and the press.

Cartoonists, especially Thomas Nast, who was famous for his Santa Claus drawings, established the elephant and donkey as symbols of American politics. What animal do you think represents you?

Hmm. I'm not really a sloth, or a mouse, or a bunny.

I draw my family:

I'm a chameleon: I fit in everywhere.

Me

Dad

Risa

Mom

Josh

Ben-Ben

Mrs. Whittam asks what we think about the class elections coming up. "Each of you should consider running. How would you help the school if you won? What would you personally bring to the job?"

Some people answer out loud, but I just think.

Next each of us makes a poster as if we wanted to run for office.

My poster:

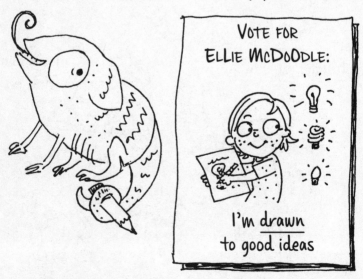

VOTE FOR
ELLIE McDOODLE:

I'm drawn
to good ideas

The FOES push me to run.

I think about it. I go back and forth. Eventually I put my name in the nomination box. The FOES cheer.

Word spreads FAST—like Ben-Ben spilling a whole bottle of Mom's waterproof black ink on a yellow rug (which he did last month).

There are lots of candidates for vice president, secretary, and treasurer.

For president there are four:

Candidate #1: Kyra

- Lets others go ahead of her in line all the time
- Gets all As and Bs
- Especially good at science
- Stands up to bullies
- Honest
- Graceful dancer

Best friend: Sophia

Candidate #2: Shane

- A joker
- Loyal to Jake
- Nice to his little sister. He carried her plus all her stuff when she fell outside the school yesterday.

Best friend: Jake

Shane poses like this a lot. I don't know why.

Candidate #3: Jake

- Deep-brown eyes
- Extra kind to classroom animals
- Tells funny jokes
- Has the nicest smile
- Plays baseball, soccer, and basketball
- A good writer
- Kind of a hero
  Best friend: Shane

Candidate #4: Me

What I hope others see:
- ~~Good~~ Best artist
- Good at thinking up new ideas
- Smiles at a lot of people every day
- Tries to be brave
- Works hard to get good grades
- Creative

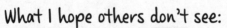

Best friend: the best anywhere, awesome Mo

What I hope others <u>don't</u> see:
- Not enough confidence
- Good artist but not great
- Clumsy
- Kind of nerdy. Or is it geeky?
- Kind of likes Jake. Has anyone else noticed?
- Crazy family

Travis cracks me up, pretending to be attacked by the cement lion. Also: the FOES are fruitalicious.

At home my family can't wait to give me advice. Some of it's good.

Mom: Be yourself. Be the best <u>YOU</u> that you can possibly be.

Dad: It's not whether you win or lose.

Risa: We need to do a makeover on you. We just need to change a few little things:

- your hair
- your glasses
- your clothes
- your personality
- the way you walk
- the way you talk

Me: That's quite a list. You're saying you have no complaints about my plain, boring toenails?

Risa: Oh, silly, simple Ellie. We'll get to your toenails eventually. There are more important things to change first.

Josh: You have to promise something big, the best thing you can imagine. Figure out how to get it later.

Me: Isn't that cheating?

Josh: Also, say bad things about the other candidates. Raise tons of money for your war chest.

Me: What's a war chest?

Josh: It's donated money to scare your opponent out of running against you.

Me: If I get any donated money, it'll be for the new playground equipment.

Josh: You could also give it to me to spend on posters that make you seem better than you are.

Me: You make politics sound disgusting.

Josh: Every politician lies. It's part of the game.

Dad: Hold up, sport—I know at least one honest and ethical politician: Senator Shepard.

Josh: How do you know Senator Shepard is honest?

Dad: I've followed her career very carefully. I've known her since she was a little kid. She lived down the street and was best friends with my sister.

Me: Wait—you know a senator?

Dad: Yes. And you'll get a chance to meet her this upcoming week at her town meeting, where she talks with residents. You and your friends can go with me if you like.

Me: YES!!!

I'm hoping to get time with Senator Shepard. Maybe she can tell me something useful.

Secrets to winning

Ben-Ben has advice for me too. He shows me how to run for president.

I draw this and put it on my blog. Ding, ding! Another "Marvelous work!" comment from Grandma Joan and Grandpa George.

There are rules for running for president, as I find out in Mrs. Whittam's class on Monday. Each candidate has to write an essay of introduction to be printed in the school newspaper later this week.

This essay is due TOMORROW!

I have no idea what I'll write for mine.

This is too hard.

I don't know what to say.

Instead I draw.

I know what I would do if I were Mo: a photo essay. Maybe I should ask Mo what she would do if she were me. Or I can just keep drawing . . .

Just before the end of class Shane stands on his desk and reads his essay to the room.

"Lice and germs, I mean ladies and gentlemen, I am so happy and honored to be listening to myself.

"I want you and me to know that I have a plan!

"If I win, I will start a new program, Principal for a Day, and I will be the first one.

"On that special day, I will start a new program entitled Superintendent for a Day, and I will be the first of those.

"On that day, I will begin a new program called Mayor for a Day, and I shall have the honor of being the first one.

"On that day when I am mayor, I shall start a new program, Governor for a Day.

"I will be the first to take on that role.

"And on that one day when I am governor I will start an event called President of the Country for a Day . . ."

The bell rings before Shane gets to Emperor of the Unknown Universe, and we leave for lunch.

Me: My dad says Senator Shepard is having a town meeting this week. You guys can come with us!

Mo: Let's all go and sit together!

Me: My dad knew her when she was a little kid.

Daquon: For real?

Me: Senator Shepard was best friends with my aunt—my dad's sister. Once they were all throwing lawn darts at a target and he missed the target and—well, um . . .

Everyone: WHAT?

Me: Well, he kind of hit her toe with the dart. She had to get rushed to the hospital.

Sitka: Okay, that's HORRIBLE. I bet she hates your dad.

Yasmeen: Ellie, you HAVE to meet the senator. Think of what a great story it would be for our newspaper!

Travis: If she hates your dad we might need a Plan B.

Sitka: And a Plan C.

Daquon: Plan B: parasail onto the roof of the capitol building.

Travis: Plan C: draw something amazing about her and post it on your blog.

In the afternoon Mr. Brendall gives us 40 minutes to either read a book or write something to put in the school newspaper. The presidential candidates, Kyra, Shane, Jake, and I, and everyone running for sixth-grade vice president, secretary, and treasurer have to work on our essays.

I'm writing a second essay. It's in verse! What rhymes with antidisestablishmentarianism?

This whole election is one big joke to Shane. I'm the only one not laughing.

I hear a few people writing funny captions for Mo's photo contest.

This is my FURniture!

But I can't listen to them. I have to do my essay.

I HAVE to do my essay. Hmm. What's Jake doing?

I don't want to work on my essay. Mo tells me to just do a crummy first draft and fix it later.

So I do. And it's a really, really crummy first draft. I'd call it a sloppy copy, a lot of rot.

I write and write and write.

The next day I write and write some more. And my essay STILL stinks!

I think I finally know what's wrong: I am not an essay kind of person. So I draw a cartoon instead of writing an essay. By the end of the day I'm happy with it.

But then I notice the other candidates' essays in the box on Mr. Z's desk.

Shane's is on top.

I'm shocked. Shane's essay is good. I redo mine.

I make it an essay so it looks like everyone else's. I also draw a little picture to go with it.

I add my essay and picture to the pile and head out.

Walking home, I have second thoughts. I should have just turned in my comic. I shouldn't have read Shane's essay. It's too late to change it now.

gurgle

The next morning Mr. Z comes to Mrs. Whittam's class and takes me into the hallway to talk. I can tell right away this isn't happy stuff about how to draw my next editorial cartoon.

"I'm afraid I have had a complaint about your running for class president while you're editor in chief. It's an unfair advantage in the election.

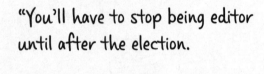

"You'll have to stop being editor until after the election.

"You can still submit writing and art to the newspaper, like any student can."

I'm going to throw up.

Did someone see me read Shane's essay?

Did I cheat?

I vote no.

I didn't copy any of his words.

But really, did I cheat? I don't know.

I practically started that newspaper. I love being editor. I didn't even <u>want</u> to run for president at first— but now I do!

Mo slips me a note:

My problems are too big to explain in a note.

In the hallway before lunch I tell Mo everything.

Me: It wasn't really cheating, right?
Mo: Did everyone else get a chance to read all of the essays?
Me: No.
Mo: It's cheating. Your conscience is bugging you because you KNOW it is cheating. And if you want me as your campaign manager you can't cheat—ever. Promise me.

Wow. She's taking this very seriously.

Me: Okay. I promise. I won't cheat again.
Mo: Good. Now, let's WIN.

I notice my stomach doesn't feel queasy anymore. I'm actually hungry.

Mo brings the FOES to my house after school. While we make a zillion signs, we also talk. It's funny, but I have to bounce my ideas off of the FOES before I really understand what I believe in.

My family gets involved:

Dad isn't the only visitor. Josh sends in a miniature me with a list of ideas for my campaign:

1. Official snack time 8:00 a.m. to 3:00 p.m.
2. Robots for teachers
3. Easy As and Bs for all
4. Train the dog to retrieve disgusting things from bathroom
5. Never mind—he already does that
6. Do Josh's homework
7. Also Josh's chores
8. Did I mention also eat all the brussels sprouts Mom puts on his plate? I meant to.
9. All prizes, benefits, and anything good reverts to Josh after a grace period of three minutes.
10. This agreement is nontransferrable.

This sounds more like a list of demands. Josh, take your weird ideas somewhere else.

The next day the FOES help put up my signs everywhere before school starts.

I rule the school—for a whopping 15 minutes.

During morning announcements, Principal Ping says student candidates are allowed to put up just FOUR signs each. That means I have about 30 signs too many.

. . . FOUR signs . . .

Does Senator Shepard ever have trouble with silly campaign rules? I wonder.

Mo helps me take down all of the extra signs at lunchtime. Then we get a surprise helper: Jake! He's already taken down six signs and folded them carefully for me.

You can save these and switch them out every few days.

Great idea!

Mglgrgle.

Cheezers! That's not even a word! Why does my brain fall apart around Jake? Josh would say it's Murphy's Law: Anything that <u>can</u> go wrong, <u>will</u> go wrong. In my life, there's an extra part to the law: If it's bad and it can get worse, it will.

The joker Shane comes along and tries to "help" too. He rips one of my signs into pieces. Jake stops him.

Jake: Hey! That is NOT cool!
Shane: She has too many!
Jake: It's not your call.
Shane: Oh. Oops. Uh. Sorry, Ellie.
Me: Mffagurgle.

Argh!!!

Hours later at home I'm thinking about Jake. If I were a princess I wouldn't wait for anyone to rescue me—not even a prince. In fact, I would be the kind who would rescue a prince. Still, I have to admit, it's really cool that Jake rescued me—TWICE!!

This picture of Jake took me two whole hours to draw and redraw and redraw. It was totally worth the time.

Jake

Jake

Jake

What is Jake's best feature? I don't know. Maybe it's EVERYTHING ABOUT HIM. He is without a doubt the awesomest guy at King Elementary. I would even say he's fruitalicious.

After dinner we go to the university for Senator Shepard's town hall meeting. Basically it's a huge empty room with lots of benches and chairs around a raised stage where the senator and her staff will sit. Because Dad works for the university, we get in early and we get good seats. We are close enough to see everything.

Cameras are everywhere!

I think up a question I want to ask the senator, so I'm glad Dad found us seats near a mic. <--(That's pronounced "mike.")

The FOES and I play Add To It:

Sit in a circle. The first person does an action. The next person repeats that action and adds another. The third person repeats the first two actions and adds another . . .

We do it until the chain of actions is impossible to remember and we're all laughing.

Meanwhile, the room fills up. I'm glad to see lots of other kids from my school.

Jake is here!!!!!!

The program starts. People are told to stand at the mics until it's their turn to ask a question.

I'm really glad to hear some short questions and short answers. It means maybe I will get a chance to ask mine.

Finally it's my turn. Butterflies take over my stomach! I swallow. My mouth is incredibly dry. Everybody is staring at me.

Don't think about Jake. Don't look at Jake.

I close my eyes—I doubt they'll ever open again on their own. Cheezers! Stay focused. I introduce myself and ask my question:

"What's the hardest thing about being a senator? I want to put your answer in our school newspaper."

The audience LAUGHS! Excuse me, that was NOT a funny question!

Senator Shepard says, "The hardest part is trying to make everyone happy, so I try to be well informed and do what I think is best."

People applaud. I don't throw up. I go back to my seat, slapping high fives with the FOES.

This will make a fantastic article for our school paper!

My guts were in my mouth.

I got photos of it!

There are some pictures of me with my eyes closed.

We can delete those.

At the end of the meeting we stand in line forever to talk to the senator personally.

She hugs Dad and then she takes her shoe off and traces the dart scar with her finger. She laughs about it. Whew.

She asks me about school and my dreams. I show her this sketch journal.

Senator: Maybe you'll run for president of our country someday.

I almost FAINT!!! Mo catches me.

Me: I'm too nervous giving speeches.

Senator: It gets easier every time. Practicing always gives me more confidence.

Me: I'm going to practice!

Senator: Please keep in touch. Send your newspaper and your blog link to my office.

All the way home I'm thinking about this: I'm friends with a SENATOR!!

Friday, the next morning, the newspaper is in everybody's hand. I flip through it to find my art. Nothing. There's NO art from me in this issue. I can't believe it!

I find my essay—they didn't run the little Vote-for-Ellie art I drew to go with it!

Cheezers. This newspaper is falling apart without me. Everyone is talking about Kyra's essay. I feel invisible.

I'm definitely not sending this newspaper to Senator Shepard. I'll wait until we have a good one.

In English class Mrs. Whittam assigns us to debate groups. Jake and I are a team, debating against Kyra and Jamian. The first thing we have to do is decide on a topic to argue about. We do a lot of arguing.

I suggest this: Should extinct animals be cloned?

It takes all my debating skills to convince them that this is the best question for our group. Luckily I am not having trouble talking in front of Jake right now. Maybe it's because I want to get a good grade so I'm concentrating hard.

Other groups' topics are: why the chicken crossed the road, and which came first, the chicken or the egg? (I don't know why chickens are so popular.)

Remember: most of your research must be from books, not the Internet.

Cloning extinct animals seems like a terrible idea to me. We've all seen movies where giant cloned dinosaurs rampage.

Jake says maybe it'd be fun to take a stand on the opposite side of what we really think. I agree, so we let Kyra and Jamian debate that cloning should not be allowed. Jake and I will argue that cloning big, scary dinosaurs (and cute, tiny ones) should definitely be allowed.

We're going to need a lot of time to work on this. Jake asks if I want to go with him to the Bubble Tea Café after school.

YES!!! my head shouts. Okay, my mouth says.

I watch the clock until school ends. We run home, then meet at my house with bikes and ride together to the café about three miles away.

We agree on this: Without weird animals, Earth would be boring. We need to bring back extinct animals—especially the weird ones. Future Earthlings will be grateful to us. They'll travel into the past to thank us, right here in this café.

We also talk about a million things:

Jake: Well, it doesn't
matter. I'm going to win.
Me: Wait—you think
you're going to beat me?
Jake: I know I am. I
know more people at
our school. You're still
kind of the new kid here.

Yikes. I was just starting to think it's easy to
talk to Jake. Now I don't know what to say. I need
to change the subject. I grab the straw from my
glass. Think fast, Ellie.

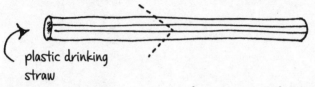

I heard if you cut a plastic straw like this and blow, you can sound like a sick trumpet.

plastic drinking straw

We borrow some scissors from the café guy and try it.

Blow here

Blatt!

Bleet!

Ha-ha-ha-ha-ha!

Jake: I'm going to win the election. The boys will vote for me. I only need to campaign to the girls.

Me: What if the boys vote for Shane?

Jake: Seriously? He doesn't even <u>want</u> to win.

Me: Then why is he running?

Jake: Just for fun.

Me: Fun? That's crazy. It's a lot of work too.

Jake asks if I want to do even more
hard work at the library tomorrow.
I float home smiling.

Saturday morning can't come fast enough!
After watching cartoons I rush to the library.
Miss Claire, the librarian, is overjoyed to see us.

Jake! Ellie!
Look what
I have!

It's our school newspaper.
Yippee. Why can't she be holding a copy of one
of the <u>good</u> issues?

Jake and I find a table in the back to work at. Our first task: come up with a team mascot, something that's extinct and should be cloned.

Dodo

Since all of the dodos are dead now (extinct), we make him into a zombie dodo.

Our next task: research our debate topic (and crack a lot of jokes).

Eventually Jake brings up a topic that is completely unfunny.

Is your election speech done yet?

We have to do a speech? Oh, man.

Before going home we promise each other to start working on our speeches tonight. Maybe if we're both writing it'll be easier somehow.

At school on Monday the campaign starts big-time. There are signs e-v-e-r-y-w-h-e-r-e.

Me: Jake has such great posters.

Mo: After all the work we did on yours, you like his better?

Me: No! I like mine! They're the best!

Mo: You're acting weird. Have you written your speech yet? Have you even started it?

Me: Oh, there's the bell. We've got to get to class!

During morning announcements Principal Ping reminds us YET AGAIN that we have to do speeches in front of the student body next Monday. Maybe Jake and I can give our speeches together.

In science class I overhear Kyra and her best friends talking about her speech and how to win the election.

Sophia: We'll make a better playground part of your platform.

(Me: The playground doesn't need a platform. It needs new stuff to play on!) (I only think this. I don't say it.)

Kyra: What's a platform?

Sophia: It's what you believe in as a candidate.

(Me: To myself: Wait! THAT'S MY IDEA! We FOES thought of that ages ago!)

I hold back my rage and very nicely inform them:

You can't make the playground your issue. It's already mine.

Well. That kind of starts a war.

You don't OWN that issue. It's everyone's.

ARGH! I don't want to argue. I want to find a better issue. Like, um . . . I think for a while. THERE AREN'T ANY. Now I'm mad.

What a good time to notice Kyra's necklace.

VOTE FOR JAKE

Me: Kyra, why are YOU wearing a sign that says Vote for Jake?

Sophia: She doesn't have to explain anything to you. Go work on your speech.

An arm yanks me.

It's Mo.

Me: They started it!

Mo: I heard the whole thing. YOU started it.

Me: They stole my issue!

Mo: You think you're the only one who noticed the playground is falling apart? I noticed it in kindergarten! Where's your speech? Let me read it.

I grab it and practically throw it at her.

Mo: Okay, this could be a lot stronger. You say "maybe" six times. Can you change that to sound more confident? And you never say you want the audience to vote for you. We need to rewrite this.

I'm thinking this is all one big gigantic pain in the neck. Who cares who wins? The important thing is, why is Kyra wearing Jake's necklace? Why don't I have a necklace from Jake? Does he like me? Does he like Kyra more? I don't really plan this. I just sort of blurt out: "I might drop out of the election."

Mo: You're thinking of QUITTING THE ELECTION? WHY? What happened? Your speech isn't that bad.

Me: It's too hard. I don't like giving speeches. Jake and I have a lot of work to do on our debate.

Mo: And?

How I feel

And—what? I'm confused. I don't know what to say, so I just make up the next part.

Me: And I want to win, but I'm under a lot of pressure. There's too much stuff going on.

Mo: Keep talking.

Me: I just . . . I'm . . . There's this . . . How do you know if someone likes you?

Mo softens.

Mo: I knew this wasn't just about the election. You know if someone likes you by how he looks at you, how he acts around you, and what words he uses. I heard that in a song. Who is it? Who are you crushing on?

Me: Nobody. It's no one. I was just wondering. It's not about me.

Mo: I doubt that. Listen, this is serious. Figure out if you're quitting the election. Call me later tonight. Don't be sad about this. We'll come up with something.

Me: Okay.

At home, Grandpa sends a message.

I love your blog and your cartoons, Ellie!

Page 77 →

Instead of my usual gushy response, I just say thanks.

What's wrong?

Then the phone rings. It's Grandpa calling to see if I'm okay. I tell him about Jake and Kyra and Mo and my speech and all this pressure.

Grandpa: Do you want to drop out of the election? Or do you want to stay in?

Me: I already gave up my editor job. I guess I should just stay in the election.

Grandpa: If you decide to stay in it, then <u>win</u> it.

I decide to test myself. If I can rewrite my speech to something good tonight, I'll stay in the election.

I'm hungry.

There's a message in the cupboard:

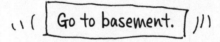

Go to basement.

So I do, and I find this:

END WOMEN'S SUFFRAGE

Ha-ha. Very funny, Josh. Suffrage is the right to vote! Suffrage doesn't mean women's suffering.

Then I notice Josh.

I'm a little shocked.

Me: What's this?
Josh: Need help with your speech?
Me: Yes.
Josh: Step right up.

Josh sits and motions for me to take the other seat. Right there we rewrite my speech from the start. I remember the good stuff from my earlier drafts, and I add new stuff that I think up plus a few things he suggests. Before I know it, we're done.

I call Mo and read my speech to her. She loves it too. It looks like I'm back in the race—to WIN!

Feeling hugely confident, I talk Josh into helping me make a bunch of little folded cards for the school cafeteria tables.

(and some as tents for Ben-Ben's toys)

In the morning Mo and I race to school early. We sneak into the cafeteria and put a sign on each table.

At lunchtime we run to the cafeteria to see the reaction. At first, it's good.

Me: I think people like them!
Mo: They make good—
Travis: Paper airplanes!

I was going to say conversation starters. The whole cafeteria is suddenly an airfield. My signs are the planes! Jake's friends are making them!

Daquon: Ellie's campaign has hit the airwaves.

I unfold an airplane to see how it's made. Here's a Jake plane:

1. 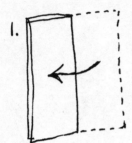 Fold a sheet of paper in half and unfold it.

2. 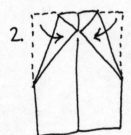 Fold the corners in until the points meet.

3. 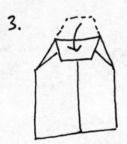 Fold the center down.

4. 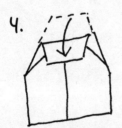 Fold the center down again.

5. Fold the center down one more time.

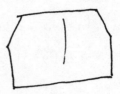

6. Flip it over.

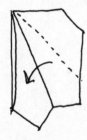

7. Fold in half.

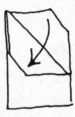

8. Fold one corner down.

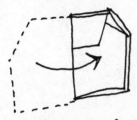

9. Fold down again.

10. Flip it over and fold the other side the same as the first side.

11. Looks like this:

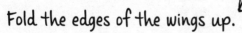

Fold the edges of the wings up.

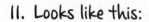

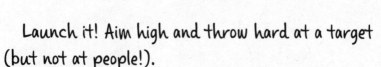

Launch it! Aim high and throw hard at a target (but not at people!).

I'm refolding a plane into a tent when the lunch lady grabs it out of my hands.

Her: Are you Ellie?
Me: Yes, ma'am.
Her: The Ellie on this card?
Me: Yes, ma'am.
Her: I expect you to pick up every single card in this room. NOW.

My rule: Never talk back to the lunch lady. She has too much power. I start picking up cards. Mo helps.

So does Jake! He gets everyone else to help pick them up also!

This isn't a surprise to me, but the next morning Principal Ping announces

No election signs in the cafeteria.

Shane points at me and laughs a super high-pitched trilling sort of bird-laugh, which makes everyone in the class laugh, including me.

When Principal Ping is done talking, our classroom debates start. Kyra begs Mrs. Whittam to let us go first (I would have been happy going last). But before we can begin, Jake and I run out into the hallway to put on our special team uniforms:

Team Zombie Dodo

Shane cheers when we come back into the room. I have to admit, it's nice having him on my side for once. Everyone else cheers too.

Kyra is wearing her Vote for Jake necklace, which makes me want to push a little harder to win the debate.

We win! Zombie Dodo will rise again!

After school Jake walks me home—my house is on the way to his.

We hang out in my backyard for a little while.

I made a fort at my house out of branches like this!

I never thought of that before!

For you, partner!

It's so cute!

Jake gives me a special gift. He even put Xs over the eyes!

Zombie Dodo goes <u>everywhere</u> with me, which means Josh and Risa razz me about it. I don't react.

At school the next day it's obvious that campaign fever has hit everyone at the same time. It's CRAZY!

I hand out little address label stickers that I draw people's pictures on.

Shane hands out insults on demand:

Jake hands out candy bracelets. How smart—every girl wants one.

I'll trade two buttons and a pencil for your candy.

At lunch Jake sits next to Kyra! I try to look away. They're laughing their heads off. Sometimes I reach into my backpack to pet my new Zombie Dodo from Jake, just to remind myself it's real.

Jake called me his partner yesterday. Maybe I am nothing special. Maybe we're just buddies. I catch a tear before it falls in my chicken.

Ryan: Ellie, don't cry. You just need better swag.

After school, instead of working on a newspaper cartoon I take down my four wall posters and put up new ones. These have special effects:

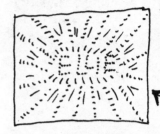

This one has glittery words on a shiny patterned background with battery-powered lights.

Look through the window.

See a better future and a new playground with Ellie as class president.

Don't be dizzy. Vote for Ellie!

If you look at it a long time, the circles seem to move.

This one says "Fly high with Ellie!" and the butterflies flutter when people walk past.

By Friday the chaos at school is <u>much</u> worse.

Want free Ice Cream Sundae Mondays?

Vote for Jake!

I'm going to vote for Jake a hundred times!

Shane's camouflage poster looks like the wall bricks. It says in very tiny letters "Vote for Shane or you're a fool in fool school."

It's genius!

Kyra's friends all wear matching shirts and hand out dozens of Kyra pencils.

see<u>K</u>
<u>Y</u>our
<u>R</u>ecess
are<u>A</u>

Shane's friends have Statue of Liberty crowns.

For freedom from tests, vote Shane!

All the girls are wearing Vote For Jake necklaces.

I pass out little notebooks I made last night.

1. paper + heavy paper

2. fold

3. staple

4. tuck in

5. done!

I don't give Jake one because he never gave me one of his necklaces.

Great! I'll use Kyra's pencil on your paper to draw signs saying Vote for Shane!

This is my very best exasperated look.

It's crazy with all the campaigning, and it's also getting ugly. Some people take the competition too far and wreck posters.

Probably Shane did this to my newest poster.

Kyra's friends aren't always nice either.

I try to ignore them. I also try to avoid Jake, but I still carry Zombie Dodo everywhere, to remind me of happier times when I thought Jake liked me.

At lunch everyone is talking about today's newspaper.

My art

The senator's town hall story written by Yasmeen is too short.

Too many comics. I drew one and so did about 100 other kids, so they're crammed in and hard to read because they're too small.

Win the election and get your old job back. The paper needs you.

This isn't as much fun as when Ellie was in charge.

Wow, that was nice of Kyra.

When I do see Jake I give him my best smile. He smiles big at me too, but then he goes and talks to other girls—especially Kyra.

I decide I've had enough of this. I'm going to show Jake that I am FUN. Any time I see a FOE in the hallway I make a big scene.

Also, I laugh extra super loud and long at all jokes that I hear, make up, or imagine.

It backfires. By the end of the day everyone is acting super energetic just like me.

Jake calls it freaky.

So much for that idea.

How am I going to get Jake to notice me? I could just go home, but instead I sit outside and think.

Jake finds me.

I take a risk.

My sister, Risa, swears that if she goes barefoot on grass it calms her and makes her feel happier. I know it sounds crazy.

Does it work? It actually kind of makes sense.

It works for me.

I like sitting here with Jake. I want to talk more. I want to ask about Kyra. I'M TOO CHICKEN! I already took a risk telling him about barefoot grass. That's enough risk for one day.

On Saturday morning I go to the library. Miss Claire has some new books for me! I'm reading when suddenly—

Jake and I laugh, maybe a little too loudly. Everyone's staring at us. Ha-ha-ha-ha-ha-ha!

Jake: What are you doing here?

Me: Reading about a girl and her brother who run away to live in a museum. What are YOU doing here?

Jake: I was just getting a book on something to make a surprise for someone.

Hmm. This could be a gift for Kyra. Should I help him? I'd still like to have him as a good friend, even if he can't be my boyfriend.

Me: I'll help if you want.

Jake: It's about butterflies.

Me: Oh! I know a field with bajillions of butterflies!

Jake: Show me!

happy ⟶   ⟵ happy too

All the way to the woods we compare our likes and dislikes. I memorize every word.

Favorite color:

Jake: Blue-green.

Me: Aqua! Same thing!!

Favorite summer trip:

Jake: Camp!

Me: Also camp!

Favorite animal:

Jake: Monkey.

Me: Zombie Dodo!

Jake changes his to Zombie Dodo too.

We get to the clearing in the woods.

It's magical.

Sitting with a hundred kajillion butterflies
fluttering around us, we talk. Mr. Z always
said, "Say the important thing up front."

I get up the courage to ask Jake
if he likes Kyra.

For some reason he
starts laughing
his head off.

It turns out . . .
Kyra is his <u>COUSIN</u>.
I let this sink in a minute.

Jake: I thought the whole city knew. Why did you think I liked her?
Me: She's been wearing your necklace every day!

Jake: That means nothing! We were at a family party and she lost a game so she has to wear my Vote necklace as punishment.
Me: Oh.

Me: Why didn't you give me one of your Vote for Jake necklaces?
Jake: I ran out.
Me: Oh.
Jake: Why didn't you give me one of your homemade notepads?
Me: I didn't think you'd want one.

I don't want him to see how happy-embarrassed-dumb-weird I feel. So I change the subject.

What's your favorite food? We both say pizza.

On Monday I'm leaving my house at the exact time Jake's walking past. Imagine that.

He gives me this!!!!

Jake: I made it for you because we're doing speeches today. Open it!

It takes me a minute to figure out how.

It's a tiny paper butterfly that unfolds.

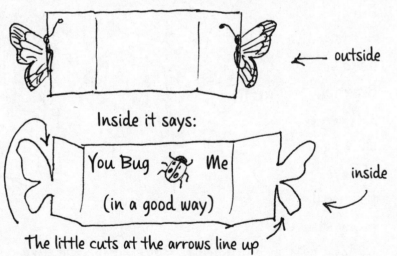

← outside

Inside it says:

You Bug Me
(in a good way)

inside

The little cuts at the arrows line up

We both laugh. This will give me all the confidence I need for my speech.

It doesn't though.

The cute butterfly necklace doesn't protect me at all from nervousness. It's speech time in about two minutes, and I'm a little shaky. Jake and Kyra gave theirs already and nobody fainted, but I can't make any promises that I'll stay standing.

Kyra and Jake grab my arms and pull me down onto a chair. Kyra shoves a water bottle into my hand.
"Drink!" she says.
I drink.

I take five deep yoga breaths.

Then I whimper, "I have butterflies in my stomach."

Jake gets in my face and says, "Ellie, picture them as our butterflies from the woods. They want you to do a good job. We all do."

I should have practiced more so this wouldn't be so scary. Three times over the weekend Mo called, asking if I needed to rehearse or memorize my speech. I kept saying I was too busy. It's sort of true—I was busy hanging out with Jake or drawing pictures of Jake or thinking about Jake.

Now it's showtime. Mo's in the audience, so she can't help. This is on me now. I go out there and . . .

I give my BEST SPEECH EVER!!!

At breakfast today Josh told me to pound the podium, so I do.

Risa said to wear my favorite shirt. It's on.

Mom said to use my special talents, so I do part of my speech with cartoony art.

Mr. Z said to say the most important things up front, so I do.

Mo said to be honest, and I am.

Jake inspired me to take a risk. My speech isn't like anyone else's.

Dad said, "Keep going until you hear the whistle." At first I thought he meant keep talking until they kick me off the stage. Dad's really saying even if there's a flag on the play, even if there's a mistake, keep going. Don't give up.

The butterflies come back, but I keep going.

Travis said be funny. Yasmeen said be quick. Daquon said use sparkle words. Sitka said bring good-luck charms.

I do all of that, and it works perfectly.

I am ambushed by hugs at the end.

That was FRUITALICIOUS!

Look who else is here!

My parents and grandparents offer to take me out for lunch, but I'd rather eat with my friends so they stay too. Weirdly, they act sweet and they don't embarrass me. (Well, the king of my daily torment and embarrassment, Josh, isn't here.)

Mom says everyone did a great job. She even liked Shane's speech:

If I win, everyone who voted for me gets a free nit comb during the next syzygy when all of the planets are on the same side of the sun.

(I have to look up syzygy, pronounced si-zi-gee. It's hard to believe, but it does exist.)

The lunch lady is trying something new. It's Bento Day! A scoop of quinoa and a California roll get plopped onto our plates. We arrange shredded cheese and fruit and vegetable pieces around it to make a picture. It's food art!

Yes, we eat like kings at King Elementary.

After lunch ends Yasmeen shows us this.

How to fold a square of paper into a butterfly:

1. 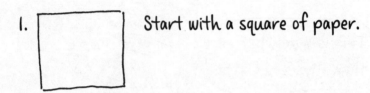 Start with a square of paper.

2. 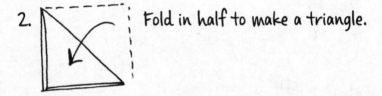 Fold in half to make a triangle.

3. 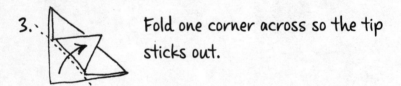 Fold one corner across so the tip sticks out.

4. 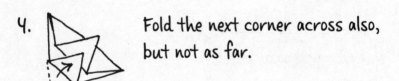 Fold the next corner across also, but not as far.

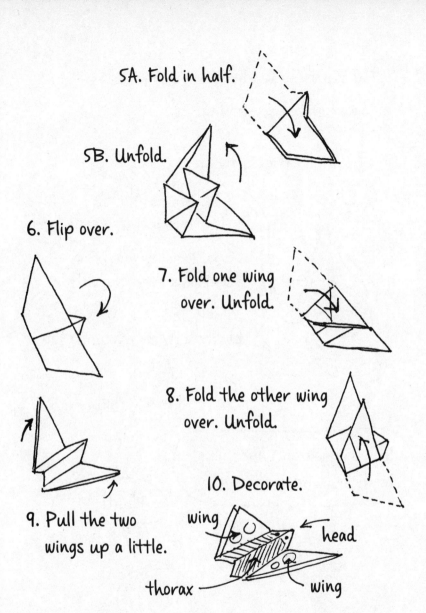

5A. Fold in half.

5B. Unfold.

6. Flip over.

7. Fold one wing over. Unfold.

8. Fold the other wing over. Unfold.

9. Pull the two wings up a little.

10. Decorate.

wing

head

thorax

wing

They don't fly very well. (We try.) But they're so cool! I make a few and give them to Jake. And that is what starts the big mess.

The rumor hose starts spraying.

Someone sees something.

It gets twisted.

It comes out in a wide spray

that soaks everyone with a

blast that isn't true or fair.

I'm a target.

Hey, are you and Jake, like, boyfriend and girlfriend?

What?

139

I try to explain. I don't think I make it much better. I mean, Mo believes me. So do the FOES. But the rest of the school? I'm not so sure they will.

I have to do two things. First: talk to Kyra as soon as school ends.

I'm scared, but I tell her the complete truth. It's <u>SO</u> awkward to say I like Jake right out loud.

My cheeks are red hot. I can barely look her in the eye. My fingers hurt from bending and pulling them so hard, over and over.

The lies about me are awful. The truth is kind of embarrassing.

I have to set the record straight though. Kyra has to know I want to win the election, but without cheating.

It turns out she heard the rumors too, and she was worried that they might be true. We're okay now. She believes me.

I'm not done though. I have to find Jake.

It turns out Jake has already gone home. I don't know his phone number or his address. I try messaging him, but he ignores me.

This is horrible. I go to bed early—not to sleep, just to lie awake half the night with a stomachache.

On Tuesday I watch for Jake to pass my house on the way to school. He doesn't.

I finally decide to run all the way to King.

Everyone stares when I walk in late to English class. The rumors must still be growing.

Kyra says hi. Actually, she practically shouts it.

Jake isn't in class.

Everything inside my head is swirling in circles. Suddenly I hear my name called from the front of the room. I don't want to leave my seat. I have to.

Mrs. Whittam has given me a couple minutes to talk about some election rumors and MY FRIEND, Ellie.

With just a few lines, Kyra clears my name. It's kind of amazing.

Word spreads fast. It looks like nobody hates me anymore. But where is Jake?

I ask Shane.

He's at home. He's sick—of YOU. Why did you start all those rumors about him being your boyfriend? Guys get embarrassed about that kind of stuff. He isn't your boyfriend anyway. He doesn't even like you. Leave him alone.

No—I—

Oh my gosh. Could Shane be right? How can I fix this?

That's all I can think of in English class. Everyone else is  voting on the ugliest-sounding word in the English language (nominees: moist, curdled, bulge, puke, uncle, fungus, and fetid, which means stinky).

The winner is fetid. Normally, I'd love this.

Say hello to Uncle Fetid!

The rest of the day is quiet torture. It would be okay to lose the election and the editor in chief job. But I can't lose Jake's friendship. That hurts too much.

Mo walks me home.

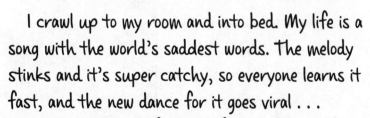

I crawl up to my room and into bed. My life is a song with the world's saddest words. The melody stinks and it's super catchy, so everyone learns it fast, and the new dance for it goes viral . . .

Bleah. Speaking of viral, I feel sick.

On Wednesday I don't want to get up. Risa pulls me out of bed by my feet and she's too cheerful about it.

> Me: Go away.
> Risa: It's Election Day!
> Me: I'll call in my vote.
> Risa: Silly. Class elections don't allow absentee ballots. Come downstairs. Dad made a special breakfast.
> Mom: If you're sick you should stay home.

I guess heartsick isn't the same as sick. I'm just so SAD I can't stand it.
Suddenly there's a knock at the door. It's JAKE!!!!!!
I want to hug him, but I hold back. Risa coaxes him inside with food.

Jake: I've been at home, sick. Shane told me what he said, so I wanted to talk with you before school.

Me: I didn't start those rumors.

Jake: I know. And if it helps, I told Shane he was wrong. Our friendship doesn't embarrass me.

Me: Oh.

Jake: Actually I like you as more than a friend.

Me: . . .

Well, I don't say anything at first. There's a surge of powerful emotion inside me, and I don't know WHAT to say. So I hiccup.

Mom gets me a glass of water.

We wolf down a few of Dad's muffins—it's a second breakfast for Jake—while my family does a goofy cheer:

Go, Ellie! Win the election!
Lead your school in a new direction!

And go Jake too!

You can tell that part was unplanned. Josh makes it work:

If Ellie can't win then I hope it's you.

Then Jake and I racewalk to get to school on time (and also because we think racewalking looks really funny).

School is like a thousand hyper speed super-electronic Ben-Ben's running all over the place. Election fever has become an epidemic. I hear Mrs. Whittam chant with Principal Ping, "Today's the last day. Today's the last day. Today's the last day."

I think we're all glad for that.

I don't have to give any speeches or write any essays or stop any rumors today. All I have to do is pay attention in class, vote at the end of the day, and celebrate that things always seem to work out in the end. (Why don't I remember that more often?)

At lunch Jake sits next to me. We don't join in the conversation much. We don't want to call attention to ourselves, but I think I am going to remember this day forever because

(we're holding hands under the table).

In science class we're making roller coasters out of foam pipe insulation and tape. We're using marbles to test friction, velocity, and forces. Mo pulls me into the hallway to work.

It's sweet that you and Jake were holding hands at lunch.

You saw?

Of course I saw. I'm your best friend. I notice things. Are you okay with today's elections?

Yeah.

I'm glad this is the end of campaigning. It's been such a roller coaster.

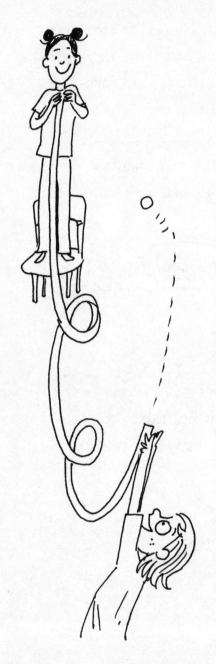

Me: I was worried earlier that you liked Jake too. You seem to smile a lot around him.

Mo: I did.

Me: Oh no!

Mo: Only a little. Since you liked him first, you get dibs on him. And he definitely likes you.

Me: You're the best friend ever.

Mo: Ellie, the whole reason I wanted you to run for president is because you're a good person and you have good ideas. YOU are the best friend ever.

Then Mr. Brendall calls everyone together to vote.

In the auditorium are five voting booths that Mr. Brendall says are the same ones used in government elections.

I know exactly how I'll vote in every race. I've thought about it very carefully. I'm just about to check off the names, but then somehow I start thinking too much and I change my mind at the last minute and . . . I vote for Jake.

I hope he voted for me. That would be the perfect balance.

☑ Jake

When I am done voting, I go into the hallway to wait for everyone else to finish.

Shane: I'm doing an exit poll. Tell me who you voted for.

Me: It's a secret ballot! I'm not telling! And that sign is disgusting.

Tonight the teachers will count all the votes. Tomorrow we will find out who won.

Me: Are you guys nervous about who won?
Kyra: It doesn't do any good to be nervous because it's already decided. We can't change it.
Shane: I'm nervous about what to be nervous about!

Jake: I just want to say, it's been fun running for president against you guys—mostly—and I like that we're all still friends.

Me: Yeah, let's do this every year. Ha!

Kyra: We should save our posters. Then it'll be easier.

Me: Save Kyra's pencils and Jake's candy bracelets too.

My bracelet has just one candy bead left. It's kind of gross now.

Laughing about how stumpy the pencils will be in a year and how disgusting those bracelets will be, we head home.

The next day is Thursday. That means it's reveal-the-votes day. Thank goodness Principal Ping gets right to it, first thing.

Kyra won by one vote. This shows how important one person's voice is.

Mo hugs me. The FOES surround me, I guess to make sure I'm okay, but really I'm fine.
I did want to win though.

Shane shouts across the classroom to Jake, "Unfair! I voted for you, man!"

Everyone laughs.
Jake says, "I voted for me also!"
Everyone laughs again.
Except me.

Jake didn't vote for me.

I voted for Jake, but he didn't vote for me.

Hey, are you okay?

Me: It's just . . . I just . . . I voted for Jake. I thought he would vote for me.

Mo: You didn't vote for yourself? Why? Didn't you think you were a good candidate?

Me: Yeah—no—yeah—I . . .

Mo: You know what this means, right? We don't know who came in second place. It could be you. That means if you had voted for yourself, you might have tied with Kyra. Then we'd have a runoff vote and you might have won.

Oh boy.

Mo: Why didn't you vote for yourself?

Me: I thought it was kind of selfish to vote for myself.

Mo: It isn't selfish. It's showing confidence in yourself. There's nothing wrong with voting for yourself! It's a good idea, if you think you're the best candidate!

Mo is being Princess Obvious right now, but I guess I needed to hear this.

Me: Wow. How could I have been so dumb?
Mo: You aren't dumb.

Mo: What would you say to me if this happened to me instead of you?
Me: I would say, "Okay, let go of that. Now, what's the NEXT best thing for us to do?"
Mo: Take your own advice, Ellie. What's next?

Hmmm.

I find Mr. Z. His classroom is chaotic too. I guess the whole school probably is.

Me: Mr. Z, I lost my election. Can I have my old job back?

Mr. Z: I'm sorry you lost. But it's STUPENDOUS to welcome you back as editor in chief! Do you want to start on Monday?

Me: I'd rather start now. We have a newspaper to put out tomorrow! I can interview Kyra for it.

Mr. Z: I think we did okay trying to do your job after you left, but it sure wasn't easy. We had really big shoes to fill.

That cracks me up.

Because really.

While I am heading back to my class, I hear a Principal Ping announcement:

> Congratulations to everyone who ran for office. In a footrace, one person wins for excellence in speed, but there can be many winners for excellence in sportsmanship. Listen now to our new sixth-grade president.

Kyra's voice comes on. She thanks Principal Ping, introduces herself, and surprises me with this:

> Thank you. I invite my competitors, Ellie, Jake, and Shane, to join my cabinet team with their great ideas.

After things settle down at the end of class I ask Kyra if we can do an interview for tomorrow's newspaper.

I hope you'll be our class historian, keeping track of our school year with a sketchbook. We could sell copies to help pay for the playground.

I'd love that!

I ask Kyra about what she wants to do as president. She has such juicy answers!

Me: What's your first goal as president?
Kyra: I want to bring people together. I want everyone to be friends again. Some of the campaigning got a little negative. I want us all to remember the good here, not the bad.

Me: How do you plan to bring people together?

Kyra: I'll get everyone working for the same goal, the new playground. It's expensive, but we can raise the money to build one. We'll have a Dime Drive, and the class who collects the most dimes gets a pizza party. We can sell recyclables and host the city's biggest garage sale and have a used books sale. I have a zillion ideas!

Plus, the people I ran against, like YOU, have good ideas. Together we can do amazing things.

Me: The best person won this race.

Kyra: Aw, thanks, Ellie!

This will be a great article for The Lion's Roar. I feel like I'm friends with a future senator.

After school we put the newspaper together. Jake isn't very cheery.

Jake: You lost the election, you're writing about the winner, and you're happy?

Me: I'm editor in chief again!

Jake: Your dad's a coach. Aren't you supposed to win at all costs?

Me: Nobody wins all of the time.

Jake: I don't know about that. Kyra wins a lot.

Me: Kyra will make a good president.

Jake: She wants me to make a time capsule to open when we graduate from high school.

Me: Just think how grown up we'll be by then. We'll be going to college. We'll know how to DRIVE! Oh! Put one of your paper airplanes in it!

Jake: And an origami butterfly too.

Jake's in a better mood now.

Mr. Z, we could raise extra money for the playground by selling message space in the newspaper. Like, if Ellie has a test I could buy an ad that says "Good luck."

Extraordinary! I guess that makes you our classified ads manager! Work with Ellie to figure out how much space we have in the newspaper for ads every week.

So the first ad that runs is this:

To E—
I thought you'd win or else I would.
I hope your weekend's super good. From J.

We finish the newspaper and send it to print. Mr. Z gathers us in a circle and says:

We definitely missed you, Ellie. I think your blood is really ink. You excel at editing.

Then he yells, "Fruitalicious!"

We all laugh and repeat, super loud, "FRUITALICIOUS!"

Someone's going to have to peel me off the ceiling because I am flying pretty high right now.

I ask Mr. Z if I can make three extra copies of the newspaper for my grandpa, Senator Shepard, and Jake's time capsule.

When it's all done, Jake walks me home. On my front porch he gives me his address and asks if I can meet him halfway to his house tonight at 7:00. He won't tell me why. Of course I say yes.

Then I say good-bye and walk into my house.

My whole family is waiting to hear about the election. I tell them I lost. They're good sports about it, mostly.

I knew this was going to happen. You lost because you didn't paint your toenails. Am I right?

Actually, I won something bigger than the election. I get to be newspaper editor in chief again!

I didn't even realize how much I wanted that job until I lost it! I would have been a good president. Kyra will be a great president. And I will be a FRUITALICIOUS editor in chief!

At dinner Ben-Ben gives me butterfly kisses.

He's fluttering his eyelashes against my cheek. It's cute!

Everyone is extra SUPER nice to me—even more than before. Finally I have to explain that I honestly am okay with not winning. Then they start teasing me again, like normal.

Oh good. Now that you're in loser mode, let's play the Opposite Game. Remember, the object is to lose. Start at the end.

At 6:55 I run-walk to meet Jake.

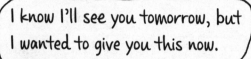

I know I'll see you tomorrow, but I wanted to give you this now.

I open the present. It's a journal!

I saw your other one is full.

 On the first page is a picture he drew because he says he wants to be in my new sketch journal, right from the beginning.

Then he kisses me on the cheek.

The end.

ACKNOWLEDGMENTS

Thank you to these and other supporters who've helped Ellie along the campaign trail:

My huge, terrific family, Jim McNally, Joan Mannino, Carol Roszka, Diane Allen, Dave Brigham, Brenda White, Diane Pendell, Peggy & Hugh McNichol, Shari Sweeney, the fabulous Bloomsbury staff, my agent, Erin Murphy, and my editors, Laura Whitaker, Caroline Abbey, and Melanie Cecka.

RUTH McNALLY BARSHAW, lifelong cartoonist, writer, and artist, worked in the advertising field, illustrated for newspapers, and won numerous essay-writing contests before becoming the creator of the Ellie McDoodle Diaries. In her spare time she studies martial arts, plays harmonica, and travels—always with a sketch journal. She lives in Lansing, Michigan, with her creative, prank-loving family. See her work at www.ruthexpress.com.